The Angry Foods

WITHDRAWN

🍵 CARAMEL TREE

Chapter 1

Fighting

All the foods sit on the table.

They are all fighting.

"I am the best!" shouts the garlic.

"You are too strong," says the tomato.

"I am the best!" shouts the meat.

"Some people don't eat meat,"
say the beans.

"I am the best!" shouts the onion.

"Not all dinners have onions,"
says the potato.

"I am the best!" shouts the mushroom.

"You smell bad," says the corn.

"I am the best!" shouts the cabbage.

"You are so fat," says the leek.

The foods fight and fight.

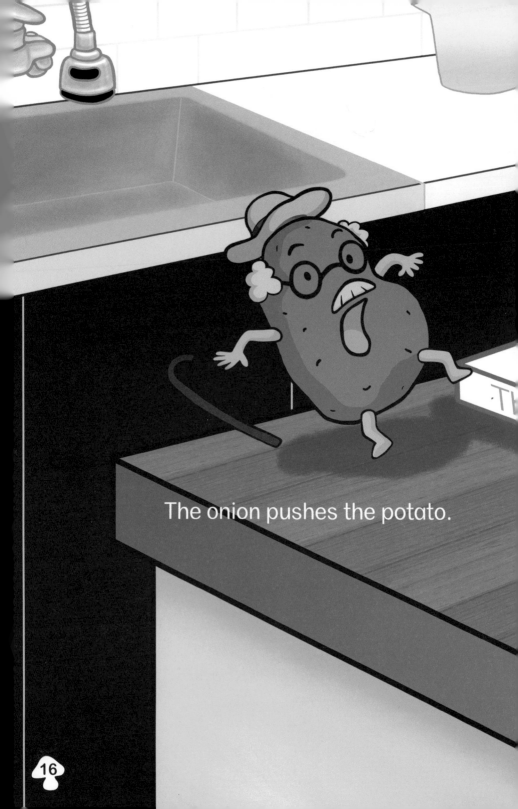

The onion pushes the potato.

The mushroom pushes the corn.

Miss Jones walks into the kitchen.

She puts all the foods in hot water.

"What is she doing?" shouts the cabbage.

"I can't swim!" shouts the meat.

"Oh, we like baths," say the beans.

"She is a bad cook!" shouts the mushroom.

"Are you hungry, Tommy?" says Miss Jones.
"Dinner is ready."

Miss Jones and Tommy sit down.

They start eating.

"Do you like the soup, Tommy?"
says Miss Jones.

34

"This soup is the best!" says Tommy.